WHERE IS ROBIN?

USA

THIS BOOK
BELONGS TO:

_____

_____

CREATED & WRITTEN BY ROBIN BARONE
ILLUSTRATED BY ROBYN MITCHELL

THIS BOOK IS DEDICATED TO
The travelers that went before me, alongside of me, and those thereafter.

ABOUT WHERE IS ROBIN?
We are a platform that uses adventure travel to teach children about the world.

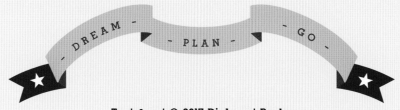

- DREAM -   - PLAN -   - GO -

Text & art © 2017 Diplomat Books
Text by Robin N. Barone
Illustrations by Robyn Mitchell
Published in 2017 by Diplomat Books

Typeset in Revers.

Printed in China.

For sales inquiries, contact sales@diplomatbooks.com.

✿ DIPLOMAT BOOKS

Diplomat Books
New York, New York

www.diplomatbooks.com

ISBN 978-0-9906310-9-5

MADE WITH ♥ IN THE USA

Up in a tree
Robin was curious to see
Every place she could possibly be.
"Don't worry Momma, I am doing this for me!"

"It's time to go! I want the world to know,
That I am looking to see its show!
Don't worry Momma, wherever I may roam
I will not forget about home!"

From City Hall above
Robin could see the City of **Brotherly love.**

Along the **Parkway** to **Boathouse Row,**
The **Art Museum** housed paintings from artists to know.

The city was founded in **1682** by **William Penn.**
Many famous advancements came later from a leader named **"Ben".**

Independence Hall was where the **Declaration of Independence** was signed.
It was a gathering place where values of freedom and liberty were combined.

The **Liberty Bell** is housed across the street.
The **Constitution Center** next door is where the past and present meet.

Next destination was the **capital** of the **United States.**

So many monuments to explore and so many dates!

Her favorite view of all was standing in front of the **White House** gates!

Off to the memorial to visit a former **president**.
She chatted about his life and what his work meant.

As the **16th President** of the United States,
Lincoln led to end the **Civil War** and slavery - very important dates.

Robin continued south to the **Outer Banks'** shore.
From atop massive sand dunes she could hear the mighty **Atlantic** roar!

This island was home to the **Brothers Wright.**
Thanks to them in **1903,** the first plane took flight.

OUTER BANKS

OBX

Over the **Smokey Mountains** and in the heart of the south,
Robin stood on the grand stage and opened her mouth.

In Nashville country musicians head to make their mark.
They sing their heart and soul all day until it's dark.

In the brilliant spotlight of the **Grande Ole Opry,**
Robin launched her country song in America's music city!

In the **Florida** heat
This bird found herself beat.
She thought a vacation in the **Florida keys** would be neat.

"This trip has got me on the run.
I think that I deserve to have some fun!
It's time to relax and enjoy the sun!"

FLORIDA KEYS

NEW ORLEANS

Then she headed north along the **Gulf Coast**
And landed in the city once a French trading post
Where **creole** was the flavor of food eaten by most!

New Orleans was the city where **Jazz** was born.
So many activities in the **French Quarter**,
Robin was torn!

SPECIALS

GUMBO

PO BOY

TEXAS

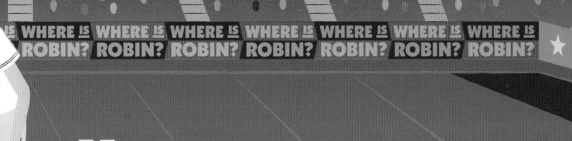

Heading west to **Texas** also known as the Lone Star state,
She visited large ranches and ate steak that was first rate,

She was invited to referee a football game
Where the players looked just like the team's name!

"What's all that noise?
It must be those rowdy cowboys!"

In the desert of the southwest,
Robin found the sunset that was the best!

Standing at the edge of the **Grand Canyon** so wide,
"If I want to get to the bottom, perhaps I should take a donkey ride!"

The **Colorado River** runs through the canyon a mile below.
How the canyon formed, scientists still do not know.

Robin continued west to the coast and landed in **LA.**
She toured **Hollywood** on such a brilliant day!

In **Southern California** the glitz of **Hollywood** took Robin by surprise.
Dreams of acting in a movie twinkled in Robin's eyes!

LOS ANGELES

CITY OF ANGELES

HOLLYWOOD

HOLLYWOOD BLVD

STAR MAPS

The **Pacific Ocean** was steps within reach.
"It's time to walk to **Santa Monica's 3rd Street promenade**
and then hit the beach!"

On the most beautiful day
Robin arrived in the city by the bay.

From the **Presidio Park** Robin stood on a ridge.
She admired **Sausalito** across the **Golden Gate Bridge!**

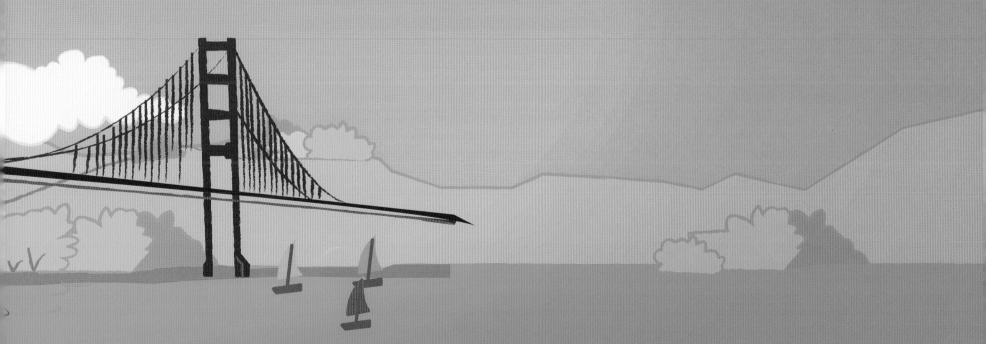

Up in the northwest
The weather was not always the best.
Why not have a coffee at **Pike Place Market** and take a rest?

The city of **Seattle** sits off the **Puget Sound.**
Sometimes people use ferries to get around!

Towering in the distance the **Space Needle** marks its place in the skyline.
The tallest structure in Seattle is also a place where you can dine.

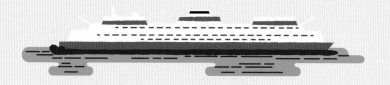

Heading to the central states and reaching the **Continental Divide,**
"These snow covered mountains are massive," Robin cried.

The capital city of **Denver** is located a mile high.
"It's hard to breathe easily," she said with a sigh!

The **Rocky Mountains** are an amazing place to ski-
Skis made for a bird - how could that possibly be?

WYOMING

In Wyoming lies **Yellowstone National Park.**
She saw all kinds of animals until it became dark!

Robin befriended a **buffalo, elk, and deer.**
She then told them about her adventures far from here.

COLORADO

LOVELAND PASS

CONTINENTAL DIVIDE

In the heart of blue sky country vast land far as she could see!
She was in a national park where animals roamed the prairie.

Washington, Jefferson, Lincoln, and **Roosevelt** are memorialized at **Mount Rushmore!**
Robin paid respect to these Presidents while hearing the mountain lions in the distance roar.

MOUNT RUSHMORE

CHICAGO

Finally she landed in a city full of light.
Many tall buildings by the lake were illuminated at night!

Chicago is the largest city in the Midwest!
Sitting beside **Lake Michigan** she planned her next quest.
"Hmm where can I find whose deep dish pizza is the best?"

In the heart of **Detroit** or **Motor City,**
Robin drove an original **Model T!**

The city is the birthplace of **Motown music** and the **assembly line.**
"Look who is performing tonight!" Robin read on the **Fox Theater** sign.

In "Beantown" or Boston,
Robin connected with early U.S. history.
This city was famous for a **Tea Party** in **1773.**

Robin headed to **Fenway Park** to watch a **Red Sox** baseball game.
This team and stadium were home to many famous athletes that sports fans could name.

The bright lights of the **Big Apple** await.
The view, restaurants, and activities are first rate!

Around **Lady Liberty** and past **Ellis Island** Robin flew.
The energy and excitement that she experienced was unlike anything she knew!

From the **Statue of Liberty, Manhattan** was within glance.
The statue was a present given to the US in **1896** from **France!**

Robin rode the subway north to midtown and exited at **Times Square.**
With all the people, lights, and activity, moments of silence are rare!

Amazed by the gathering of activity at **42nd Street** and **Broadway,**
Robin bought a ticket to a musical for that very same day!

"There she is! It's my Robin!
My dear child, where have you been?"

"Momma, I have traveled this country and it is so great!
Now I am ready to see the world, I must set a date!"

Follow Robin's other adventures!

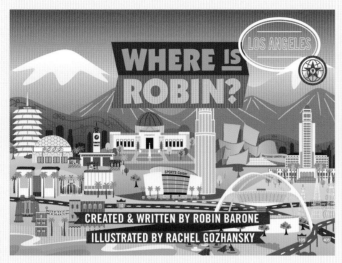

Where is Robin? Los Angeles
ISBN: 978-0-9906310-8-8

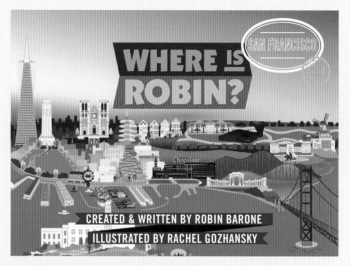

Where is Robin? San Francisco
ISBN: 978-1-946564-06-1

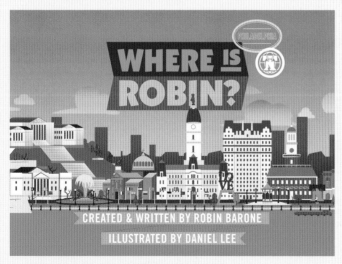

Where is Robin? Philadelphia
ISBN: 978-0-9906310-5-7

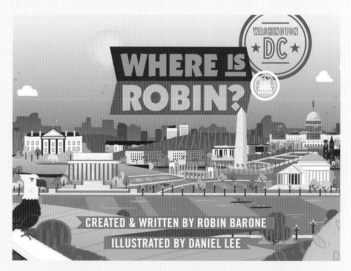

Where is Robin? Washington D.C.
ISBN: 978-0-9906310-6-4